Dedicated to my sister Brandy
and her beautiful children;
Kayla, Khloe, and Piper.

My Mama is a Rock Star

Crystal Bowersox

Copyright © 2022 Crystal Bowersox

All rights reserved.

ISBN-13: 979-8-3521-9239-9

My mama is a rock star.
She's bold and strong and brave.

And when I'm feeling scared at night, she helps my heart feel safe.

She's been to many places.
She's traveled far and wide.

And though she's traveled 'round the world, her favorite place is by my side.

My mama is a rock star,
she loves to sing her songs.
I miss her when she goes to work
but she's never gone too long.

I love to watch her change the
strings on the pink guitar she plays.
And sometimes when she asks me to
I join her up on stage.

My mama is a rock star.
She shows me that I can
achieve my dreams,

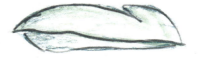

walk on moon beams
if I work hard and plan.

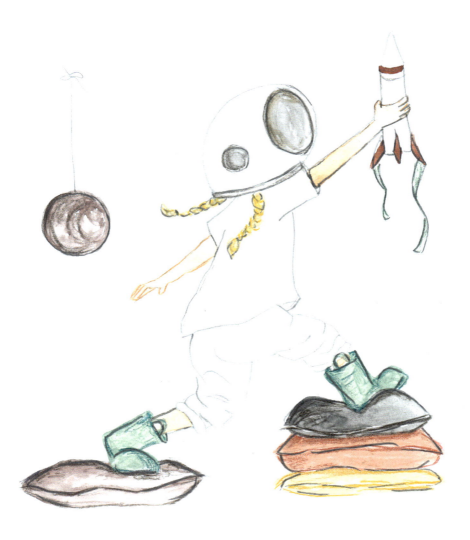

She tells me that I'm special
and there's no one else like me.

We sing and dance,
and play and prance!
We let our hearts fly free!

She likes to teach me lots of things,
like how to knit and pearl.

And that I can do anything,
because I am a girl!

Someday I'll be a rock star in oh so many ways.

Because I know she loves me so,
and that will never change.

ABOUT THE AUTHOR

Born and raised in Northwest Ohio, Crystal Bowersox is an American singer-songwriter, independent mom, Type One Diabetes advocate and now, author. She has been a nationally touring artist since placing 2nd on American Idol in 2010.

In 2022, Crystal became a mother of two after choosing to adopt her niece, Piper, following the loss of her sister. She was inspired to write this story to exemplify the ability of women to pursue their passions while simultaneously creating loving homes.

For more information, visit crystalbowersox.com

Made in the USA
Middletown, DE
11 November 2022

14412769R00018